Kate Larkin,
the Bone Expert

Kate Larkin,
the Bone Expert

Lindsey Tate

illustrated by
Diane Palmisciano

HENRY HOLT AND COMPANY
NEW YORK

Henry Holt and Company, LLC
Publishers since 1866
175 Fifth Avenue
New York, New York 10010
www.HenryHoltKids.com

Library of Congress Cataloging-in-Publication Data
Tate, Lindsey.
Kate Larkin, the bone expert / Lindsey Tate ; illustrated by Diane Palmisciano.—1st ed.
p.   cm.
Summary: When Kate breaks her arm, she learns all about bones,
from how X-rays work to how bones heal, and by the time she gets her cast removed
at the end of the summer, she is an expert. Includes related activities and glossary.
ISBN-13: 978-0-8050-7901-2 / ISBN-10: 0-8050-7901-7
[1. Bones—Fiction. 2. Family life—Fiction.] I. Palmisciano, Diane, ill. II. Title.
PZ7.T21127Kat 2008   [Fic]—dc22   2007027588

First edition—2008
Printed in the United States of America on acid-free paper. ∞
1 3 5 7 9 10 8 6 4 2

With all my love to James,
to Sophie, and to Antonia,
whose broken arm was the
inspiration for this book

—L. T.

To the memory of my mother

—D. P.

CONTENTS

CONTENTS

One

Bones, Bones, Fascinating Bones

I never really thought about my bones before last summer. They were just something inside my body that I took for granted. I was much more interested in dinosaur bones and turtle shells and the glow-in-the-dark skeleton costume that my cousin Jamie wore for Halloween. Then, last July, I broke my arm and became something of a bone expert. When I grow up maybe I'll even be an *orthopedist*—that's a special word for bone doctor.

My name is Kate Larkin and I just turned eight years old. Most of the time I live in New York City, but I spend every summer at my grandma's house in the country, and I love it there.

My favorite things in the world are climbing the giant oak tree in the backyard, doing scientific experiments with my big sister, Eliza, and whirling along the path by the river on my bike. My mom says I keep her on her toes

because I am always on the go. Now I know that I couldn't do any of these fun things without the help of my bones—there are over 200 of them in our bodies (206, to be precise) and they each have a job to do.

Together, all our bones form our skeleton. This supports our body's weight and gives it shape. The skeleton

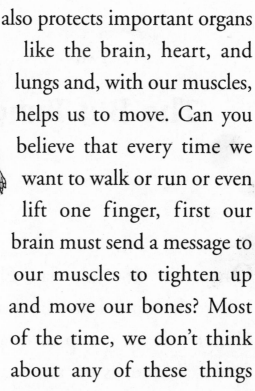

also protects important organs like the brain, heart, and lungs and, with our muscles, helps us to move. Can you believe that every time we want to walk or run or even lift one finger, first our brain must send a message to our muscles to tighten up and move our bones? Most of the time, we don't think about any of these things going on inside our bodies. It can take a broken bone to make us pay attention, which is exactly what happened to me last summer.

Two

The Big Bang

One really hot July day, Eliza and I were heading into the house for dinner when a group of dragonflies darted around us on rainbow wings. We ran with them, our wet towels stretched out behind us, swooping barefoot across the lawn. It was fun to fly, but then I rounded a corner too quickly and slipped. I didn't have a chance to put down my hands to soften my fall, and I crashed onto the top of my arm. All the air rushed out of me, and I lay in the grass, looking up into the trees, waiting to see if I was hurt. Then the pain in my arm

7

started, sort of throbbing as if someone was banging a drum near my shoulder.

I must have screamed loudly, because my mom shouted my name and I heard her running across the grass. She and Eliza loomed over me, Eliza quiet, my mom full of

questions—"Are you okay?" "Where does it hurt?" "Can you get up?"— none of which I could answer. My arm was aching like crazy.

Mom scooped me up and carried me inside to the sofa, where I lay crumpled in the cushions. I started to shiver, so Eliza ran upstairs for clothes and a blanket while Mom slipped off my wet swim things. I closed my eyes and tried not to breathe, hoping the pain would go away.

"I don't know for sure," Mom whispered, "but I think you've broken your arm. We need to get to the hospital to have it checked."

She helped me into my favorite
skirt, but putting on the top was
impossible. I couldn't lift my arm, so
Eliza put the blanket around my
shoulders instead. "You look green,"
she said. I felt green—hot and cold
and shivery.

We were waiting for Grandma Pam. She had taken the car to go grocery shopping. It seemed like we waited for hours, but she told me later that she sped back from the store in less than four minutes after Mom called her. She rushed out of the car, took one look at my arm, kissed my head, then got right back in. I sat on Mom's lap in the back.

"Daddy will meet us at the hospital," Mom said. "He's coming straight from the office."

I remember every bump in the driveway down to the main road, because with every movement, my arm hurt so much. Usually the rabbits on our lawn run helter-skelter into the woods when the car sets off, but that night they sat, ears up, watching our slow progress down the driveway. I leaned into the soft warmth of Mom, wondering what would happen next.

In my bedroom in New York, I have a model of a stegosaurus. Daddy and I put it together, bone by bone, building up the skeleton from the smallest plates on the end of its tail to the skull. The plastic bones are glossy and white, and as I sat in the car, that is how I imagined the bones inside

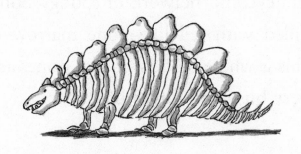

my body. I pictured one snapped in two, broken in a perfectly straight line—smooth, white, and solid, inside and out.

I now know that bones are not like this at all. Instead, they are living parts of our bodies, filled with cells, nerves, blood vessels, and minerals. The outside of a bone is hard and solid, but the inside is different. It's a honeycomb network of spongy bone filled with jellylike bone marrow—this is where blood is made. Bones are very busy and full of life.

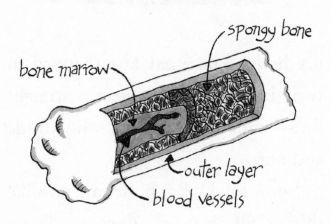

spongy bone

bone marrow

outer layer

blood vessels

Three

Emergency Room Blues

I had never been to a hospital before, and, as the automatic doors swung open in front of us, I felt nervous. Mom explained to me that it was too late in the day to see a regular doctor, but that the emergency room was open all day and night, and people went there for all sorts of reasons.

"The last time I was at an emergency room," she said, "you weren't even born. Eliza was two and slipped in the bath and cut her chin. She was fine, and you will be too."

It was busy inside. A nurse brought a wheelchair over to us, so that Mom could sit with me in her lap and fill out lots of papers. Eliza and Grandma Pam played games of War in the waiting area, and I wished I were playing too. I nestled into my blanket and looked at the other people there, trying to guess why they were at the hospital. I kept very still. My arm hurt when I moved.

Then I heard my name being called. My stomach turned over. I was scared because I wasn't sure what would happen next. "Here we go," said Mom.

Eliza and Grandma Pam had to stay in the waiting room. They waved to us as we went through big doors into an area called *triage*. It made me think of the tree house in the backyard, and I wondered when I would climb a tree again. Mom said that triage is a way of making sure that the sickest people get to see the doctor first. A nurse took my temperature, glanced at my arm underneath the blanket, and

asked questions. "How did it happen,
honey?" I let Mom tell her. I felt dizzy.
There were too many people and the
lights were very bright.

The nurse wheeled me to a bed, a kind that moves up and down. She cranked it to its lowest level so Mom could slide me onto it, and then raised it pretty high. It felt good to lie down, but I wished Mom was still holding me because my arm was hurting again.

I could see everything from my perch—a girl sleeping in the bed across from me, doctors and nurses hurrying by with clipboards. Then I saw Daddy with Grandma Pam and Eliza. He made it. "How's my big girl?" he asked, and gave me a gentle hug.

Four

X Marks the Spot

It seemed like we did a lot of waiting at the hospital. Grandma Pam and Eliza came over to my bed to say good night. They were going home.

"You're so brave," said Grandma Pam as she kissed me.

"You're lucky," said Eliza. "You get to stay up late." I wanted to go home with them and curl up in my own bed, but of course I couldn't—not yet anyway.

Daddy held my hand. "Close your eyes. Try to sleep," he said, and Mom stroked my hair. Sometimes they told me stories about when they were little, but mostly we were quiet, just waiting. Finally, a doctor arrived. She pulled curtains around my bed to make a little room.

"Hi, I'm Dr. Feldman," she said. "I'm a special bone doctor for children—a *pediatric orthopedist*." She looked at my chart, then at my arm, and wheeled me off in my bed. "Time

for X-rays," she said, and smiled. She had a friendly smile.

"Hi, I'm Mark," said the X-ray man. He explained that he wanted to take two X-rays to find out if my bone was broken. "It won't hurt," he said. But I knew this already from having X-rays done at the dentist. "I'll have to move your arm a little to put it in the right position," he added. I didn't like the sound of that. "Don't worry," he said. "I'll be careful."

The X-ray machine was big, with parts that Mark slid up and down. Being so close to it made me curious. "How do X-rays work?" I wanted to

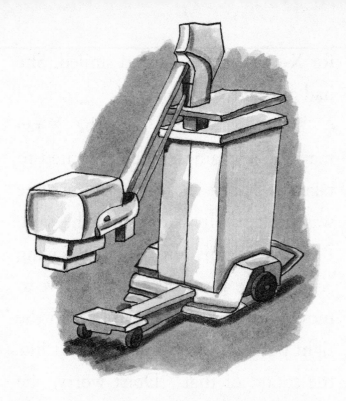

know. Both Mom and Daddy laughed. I guess not even the pain in my arm could keep me from asking questions.

Mark told me that an X-ray machine sends out invisible waves of energy called *radiation*. "X-rays go through our bodies like sunlight through a window, but they can't pass through bones or teeth. That's why your bones will show up as white outlines on the X-ray film, a little bit like shadows."

I gripped Mom's hand while Mark moved my right arm into position. It hurt, and I cried out but just for a second. "I need to put this around you," he said. It was an apron, the kind at the dentist's office. "It's made of lead, and radiation can't pass through it," Mark said. "It will protect the rest of your body."

Mark and my parents stepped outside the room. Through a window,
I saw Daddy give me a thumbs-up
sign, then I heard the X-ray machine
beep and a light flashed. We took

two X-rays and then we were done.

While we were waiting for the films to be developed, Mark told me that X-rays were discovered more than one hundred years ago by a German scientist named Wilhelm Roentgen.

"It was an important discovery," he said. "Before X-rays, doctors couldn't see inside the human body, but now we have a map of what's going on under the skin. No more guesswork."

With the X-ray films in his hand, Mark looked serious. He slowly pushed my bed back to my little curtained room. "Is it broken?" asked Mom. He nodded. "The doctor will explain everything," he said. "Good luck, Kate," he added and gave me a smile and a strawberry lollipop. It felt strange to hold it in my left hand instead of my right.

Five

Humerus Doesn't Mean Funny

From my hospital bed, I could see a dark patch of sky and I knew it was past my bedtime. Dr. Feldman came back. She had the X-ray films in her hand. I didn't want to hear what she was going to say, as if somehow that would stop my arm from being broken. I counted the stars and tried to ignore the whirling in my stomach.

Dr. Feldman held up the X-ray films to show my parents. I couldn't stop myself from looking. It was fascinating to see inside my body. There

was a crack running across a bone, and one part of the bone was sticking out like a dog's tail. I felt sick.

"Kate, you have broken your *humerus*, the big bone between your elbow and your shoulder," said Dr. Feldman. "It's a simple fracture," she continued. "Look. The bone is broken straight across." She pointed to the X-ray. "There are different kinds of breaks: a *compound* fracture, where the bone breaks through the skin; a *hairline* fracture, where the break is like a crack; and a *greenstick* fracture, where the bone breaks on one side but does not break all the way across. They all take different amounts of time to mend. But, luckily for you, arm bones heal faster than leg bones," Dr. Feldman said.

"Bones mend on their own," she continued, "but my job is to make sure that the new bone grows straight. We're going to put a cast on you now to hold the bone in position while it heals."

My cast was made of bandages soaked in plaster. It felt cold, wet, and heavy all at the same time. It dried

quickly and was soon hard. The throbbing pain in my arm had quieted down
and become just an ache.

"How long will she wear the cast?"
Mom asked.

"About six weeks," Dr. Feldman said, "but we'll probably change the cast in a few weeks to a lighter one, maybe even a glow-in-the-dark cast." She gently touched my chin and smiled. "I need just one more X-ray to make sure the bones are straight inside the cast, and then you can go home."

My X-rays must have been fine, because soon after that Dr. Feldman signed some papers to let us leave the hospital.

Six

Let the Healing Begin

We walked outside into the darkness. Now that we were away from the light and noise of the hospital, I was really tired. The weight of my cast pulled me sideways. Daddy carefully picked me up. "You were a trouper," he whispered. "Let's get you home." I started to cry. I felt as if I had been holding my breath the whole time I was at the hospital.

Mom and I sat together in the back of the car, and we drove home in silence. It was past midnight. As we turned to go up our driveway, we saw a mother deer standing with her fawn. They stared at us, sniffing the night air, then turned and dashed into the woods.

As I fell asleep that night, Daddy sat by my bed. He held my hand and told me that bones are amazing and already my bone was starting to heal itself. He said a blood clot would

close up the broken ends of the bone
while I was asleep, and then, in the
morning, new bone cells would start
to build a bridge between the two
ends of broken bone. He talked about

two kinds of bone cells—*osteoblasts* and *osteoclasts*—and in my sleepiness I saw them as busy ants. One group, the osteoblasts, would build new bone from one side of the break to the other, while the osteoclasts would dissolve sharp edges of broken bone. I dozed off thinking about this hum of activity going on inside my body.

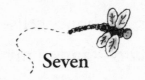

Seven

Fun Things to Do While Wearing a Cast

"I wish I could have a cast," Eliza said in the morning, and she signed her name on it in big letters while I was still in bed.

All I could think about were the things I wanted to do but couldn't, like swim, ride my bike, and climb up into the tree house. Getting out of bed was almost more than I could manage. It took at least twenty minutes of inching across the mattress on my back, Mom coaxing, me crying, until finally I reached the edge of the bed and slumped onto my feet. I was miserable.

"Let's make a 'Can Do' list," suggested Grandma Pam over the sizzling sound of bacon and eggs on the griddle. We sat there thinking about things I would still be able to do and came up with some good stuff that she wrote down—going on nature walks, doing science experiments, drawing, doing puzzles, playing with

the dollhouse, painting, baking, watering the wildflower patch, putting on shows, and going for ice cream with Eliza (that was Eliza's idea).

The first few days after I broke my arm, it seemed like my arm was in charge and nothing was easy. I walked with a stoop, my cast pulling me forward. It was difficult to stand up from sitting, so I learned never to sit on the floor, and getting out of bed was still painful.

I felt like a dragonfly caught in a net. There were only two pieces of clothing I could wear—my favorite pull-on skirt and a tank top with loose straps that slipped easily over my cast. This was fine with me, but Mom cut up a few of my T-shirts to make their armholes bigger. Eliza did the same with a couple of her own and made a cast out of old bandages. Grandma Pam called us ragamuffins.

 **Eight**

Countdown to Cast-off . . .

Little by little, things got easier. I learned to draw with my left hand and got pretty good at it. I dressed the dolls in the dollhouse with just one hand by leaning them against my cast. I discovered that if you look closely at a patch of grass, it's full of insect life, even tiny frogs, and I filled pages of

my nature journal with drawings of
what I saw. I made dinner with
Grandma Pam every night, adding
herbs from the garden, mixing ingre-
dients, and setting the table on the
porch. One Saturday, Daddy and I put
on a show in which I played the part
of a cat with a broken leg and he was a
bluebird.

We had lots of visitors those first few days, including my aunt and uncle and cousins Tom, Jamie, and

baby Rosie. Everyone wanted to sign my cast and hear about my visit to the hospital. I loved being the center of attention and listening to everyone's stories about broken bones. But when all the talk got to be too much, I watched Rosie in her bouncy swing and wondered about her little bones. Mom told me that babies are born with soft bones called *cartilage,* which is very flexible. As they grow, their bones become harder until there are only a few bits of cartilage left, like in the tip of the nose and in the ears.

Every week, I went to see Dr. Feldman in her office to check that my bone was healing well. She took an X-ray and looked at my cast. The first week she told me to drink lots of milk so that calcium would go into the new part of my bone. "Calcium is a mineral that makes bones hard," she explained. She even told me that if a bone were soaked in vinegar, all the minerals would be removed, and the bone would become so soft that it could be tied in a knot like spaghetti. After that news, I drank my milk at breakfast and bedtime— and so did Eliza.

One day when my skin was itching like crazy under the cast, and all I wanted to do was jump in the swimming pool, Daddy brought a ladder out of the shed and leaned it against the oak tree. "Climb carefully," he said, then watched me clamber up

into the tree house. It felt good to be there in the shade among the birds, drawing, far from the sound of Eliza splashing in the pool.

Three weeks after my break, I got some good news from Dr. Feldman. My bone was mending well and I could get a new cast, a lighter one. Off came the old cast in a cloud of dust. Dr. Feldman used a special saw, a little like a pizza cutter, and it really tickled. For a moment I saw my arm—it looked pale, thin, and scaly—but then the new cast was on. Dr. Feldman squeezed it tightly onto my arm so it wouldn't slip off when it dried. It was yellow, and it really did glow in the dark. I liked it.

Some days, with the new cast, I forgot that my arm was broken. But other days, I really wanted to ride my bike and swim, and those were still on the "no" list. I would sit down and cry, and fight with Eliza. So Mom would read to me, or send me up the ladder into the tree house, or I would put a plastic bag on my cast and make mud pies and strange-smelling perfumes out of flowers.

Nine

Ready to Ride

Finally, before we went back to the city in September, it was time to have my cast removed. I was excited but also a little nervous. Just one more X-ray, then Dr. Feldman would decide for sure. I knew the routine for my X-rays. Jenny, the office radiologist, didn't even have to tell me what to do. She just checked that my apron was on properly and went out of the room to turn on the machine. "Is today the big day?" she asked. I nodded, hoping my bone looked good enough in the picture.

It must have, because Dr. Feldman was smiling when she came into the room. "Well, it looks like your bone has done a great job healing," she said. "It's time to take off the cast." She got out a little electric saw, and it whirred across my cast. It was a funny feeling, and it matched the butterflies in my stomach. I remembered the scaly arm I had seen when my first cast was

removed. Then it was off. I stared at my right arm. It looked like a twig, skinny with peeling dry skin. Maybe the cast had squeezed it too much.

"Don't worry," Dr. Feldman said,

"it's just because you haven't used the muscles for a while and so they've become smaller and weaker. They'll soon be back to normal." She showed me how to circle my arm around and swing it back and forward to help the muscles get stronger. I could move my arm again! "That'll make your arm strong, that and lots of playtime."

Dr. Feldman put her finger on the spot where the arm was broken. "You'll feel a bump here," she said. My mom touched it and nodded. "It's called a *callus*. It's the new part of the bone." She showed it to us on the X-ray film. It looked like a bulge. Dr.

Feldman explained that it would be there for a while, because the process of mending the break was still going on. "Osteoblasts continue to create new bone cells while the osteoclasts wear down the unneeded part of the callus until the bone is straight and smooth."

I had just one last question. "Can I ride my bike?"

Dr. Feldman laughed and said, "Yes, but not at full speed yet. Wait two more weeks for that." I gave her a hug but I couldn't lift my right arm around her so it was a funny one-armed hug.

Ten

Racing Along the Riverbank

That afternoon, I took my first bike ride after breaking my arm. How nice it was to be wheeling along the riverbank with Mom and Eliza just behind! I was aware of things I had never noticed before. I sensed the different parts of my body working together, muscles and bones sending

messages back and forth from my brain to work out how to ride a bike. I was thinking about all the amazing things that my body can do, and how I would never have learned about bones if I hadn't broken my arm, when Eliza sped past me on her bike. But it didn't bother me one bit. I had a mended broken arm and I felt great. And I had a fantastic story to tell my friends about how I spent my summer vacation.

KATE'S JOURNAL

Here are some experiments and activities you can try at home.

Chicken Bone Experiment

This is an experiment that my dad showed me. It made me drink my milk!

The next time you eat chicken save a few thin bones, like the wishbone and the wing bones. Wash them and let them dry. Put some bones in a jar filled with vinegar and the rest in a jar filled with water. Leave the bones for about a week

vinegar

water

(you might have to add new vinegar every couple of days). At the end of the week, take out the bones. Try to bend them. You should find the bones that were in vinegar have become completely bendable!

⏰ after a week: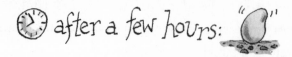

This is because the acid in the vinegar breaks down the calcium carbonate in the bone. Calcium carbonate makes the bones solid—just like calcium makes the bones in your body solid. Now I bet you'll drink your milk too, because it contains lots of calcium to keep your bones strong.

Egg Experiment

Calcium makes eggshells hard as well. You can do the same experiment with a hard-boiled egg. Put the egg in vinegar and watch. Little bubbles will appear all over the egg. A few hours later the vinegar will have broken down the whole hard shell, and you'll be left with just a wobbly egg.

vinegar

⏰ after a few hours: "🥚"

Rose Petal Perfume

This was one of the things I liked to make when I couldn't go swimming or bike-riding. When roses start to lose their petals, you can put the petals in a pan of water. I like to use rainwater that I've collected but any water is fine. Ask an adult to simmer the roses and water on the stove for a few minutes. When the water has cooled down, strain the rose petals until you are left with rose petal perfume. It smells good for a few days. Red roses make a pink perfume. Yellow roses make a brownish perfume.

How to Make Mud Pies

I made mud pies whenever I felt frustrated about what I couldn't do with a broken arm. Mixing the mud always made me happy—and dirty. I was supposed to cover my cast with a plastic bag, but I often forgot, and my cast got pretty muddy by the end of the summer. But it didn't stop my arm from healing.

Put some soil in a bowl (make it an old bowl unless you want your parents to get mad) and add  a little water. Mix it together with your hands or an old spoon. Keep adding water until it gets as squishy as you'd like. It's fun to make pretend food or mud castles. They will bake hard in the sun. I once made a house for worms.

GLOSSARY

blood clot. A solid clump of blood cells that seals wounds and stops them from bleeding.

bone marrow. A thick spongy jellylike tissue inside bones that makes blood cells.

calcium. A mineral that bodies need to make bones strong.

callus. A lump that forms when two ends of a broken bone join and mend.

cartilage. A soft flexible material that turns into bones as babies grow. Adults still have cartilage in a few places, including their noses and ears and between joints.

cast. A bandage that protects a broken bone while it's mending.

emergency room. The unit, or area, of a hospital that treats sudden accidents or illnesses. It is open all day and night.

fracture. When a bone breaks, it is called a fracture.

humerus. The long bone in the upper arm between the shoulder and the elbow.

lead apron. A heavy apron made of lead that blocks radiation and protects the body during X-rays.

orthopedist. A bone doctor.

osteoblast. A cell that forms new bone.

osteoclast. A cell that breaks down bone.

pediatric orthopedist. A bone doctor who treats children.

radiation. Invisible waves of energy given off in the form of rays.

radiologist. A doctor who takes X-ray pictures, then reads and makes sense of them.

triage. A way of sorting patients at a hospital to make sure the doctor sees the sickest patients first.

X-rays. Pictures taken by a radiologist or technician of the inside of a body.

X-ray machine. A machine that takes X-ray pictures.